Pieces of ink

Anneli Sundqvist

Förlag: BoD - Books on Demand, Stockholm, Sverige
Tryck: BoD - Books on Demand, Norderstedt, Tyskland
ISBN: 978-91-8057-483-9

Table of contents

Pieces of ink

Old ‘man’ do

The death is following after

your steps

step by step it closing in?!

and you know that is true

we all do

soon you feel the death

like a breath... in your neck?!

what can an old ‘man’ do

Our time

I was like a flower
I was flowering when you were
by my side.
but you left, and me I fade away
from your sight.
you were my sun and now
you gave me the rain.
it made me mature, with time
but I will miss your love every day.
but love goes on with or without you
I just want to say
thanks for our time.
I loved every day

The breeze

When the wind blow
through my hair
I feel the breeze, the touch of
a cool summer day, into my
hair
what a wonderful feeling
I thinking for myself
there on the walk in the cool
summer day

Toe into the water

Sorrow is
like the blue waves
from a sea
the washes up on your shore
when you dip your toe in the
water… cold
you know… of
cold water… you can’t swim in it
maybe you drowning from the
waves of the sea
we see if you are alive
tomorrow day
sorrow is a hard thing to deal

Carved into your heart

The summer laying

In front of your eyes, so open

your eyes.

its waiting for you to make

this living

of all this summer days.

so, take care of your summer day

summer fast passing by but

the

memories of this summer

may it be left into your heart

let the summer of' today' be

carved

into your heart

Spread your wings

The fantasy can make you
fly
give you wings
so, to learn to spread your
wings
you must take care of
your fantastic mind
use it
and fly away... for a while.
we all need it
sometimes

Blue' waves

Sea, the ocean
always give a kind of sad
and lonely
feeling of the blue waves.
all these feelings inside
leave a loneliness into the
depth of the heart
that is the sea, ocean.
and on the shore footprints in
the warm sand that
disappears after a while. As
the days disappears too
down into the horizon line.

Until tomorrow

Please tomorrow
don't come yet
I'm not ready for that

I laying in my bed
trying to get some sleep
in my head

my brain is on, on on...
and my eyes are tired

I can't find any rest
into my mind, will I be
awake until tomorrow?

I wish one dream

will come along

even if it’s in the late hours

of the night

I understand

it be no rest tonight

so

I lying awake until

tomorrow.

Like sweetest honey

A romantic danger
In a good way when we come together.
a fire spark' into the eyes
and a little smile
you are mature so, you play
well with fire.
perfume is in the air a scents
of a flower.
step by step come closer
look into each other's eyes
and come alive.
with colourful clothes
you dressed yourself up for this
night.
today you talk so sweet, you
choose your words well and
you talk like the sweetest
honey.

Horribly hours

I laying in my bed

head on the pillow and feet

under the quilt in my bed

I slept just some broken hours

the dreams were not here to

night

feel bad and blue

eyes so tired

want to shut my eyes

but I can’t

Oh!

what a horrible hours

Golden beach

Barefoot children
in different ages
running in the sand, put their
toes
into the waves...
little children you have
something that not can be
bought with money
it's this peace in your souls
and your young age.
I hope you all have something
to remember, a lot of happy
memories
of soulful days of
your younger days
so, when you need you can
pick them up
one by one
like this beautiful
memories of the days
on the ...
...golden beach

Love and passion

Love and passion

red roses and perfume

beautiful eyes

and red dresses

a date in the night,

and a spark' into that night

lead to family life, sometimes.

or just a loneliness into

the night

and fade red roses

after

a lost and gone romance'

myself

When I look myself into the
mirror
it isn't about how I look today
that I am looking for
it more about
how I feel today
when I take a closer look into
the reflection in the glass
I see deep inside.
so, when I take this closer look
into my eyes, I see
these eyes are brighter than before
I feel so good with myself
it's something inside
something inside I started to love today
and it's the person in front
of me
its
myself

The loving light

Creatures of the night
is creeping into the dark
dig a hole in your soul
deeper and deeper
this horror and pain
it hides into the darkest shadows
of your mind.
dark thoughts find no peace
afraid of the light
only salvation is to step
into 'the loving light'
but they do not dare, to be seen.
afraid of not be loved
for who they be.
so, they creep away from the light
into the dark shadows of your
mind
fare away from salvation
'this loving light'

Someday

You see
life just driving through
in the other line
when you standing in the corner
you waiting patiently
someday you will take
that step into life.
give everything you have
love with all you have
but not now, you do not dare.
not yet
you are not ready yet
but life is living
and you are not even close today.
but you waiting patiently
thinking
'maybe someday'

(maybe tomorrow day ?!)

Strong heart

To get a strong heart

then we must use it

'pump it up'

use it

Target

A poet, I am, a simple one
writes I put down in ink
one by one...
for someone
who like to read
my letters and words
a story to read
everyone.
maybe fun for someone
maybe it hit you in your heart
that's my target
but, I'm just... a simple poet
so, I guess I miss my target

Ocean talk

The shore

so beautiful only eyes can see.

you hear the ocean talk

with its bruising's waves into

this stones and sand.

when you walk on the shore

barefoot and leave...

...only footprints after you

is left on this beach.

and a deep memory of

freedom inside your soul

you keep

Tones of a harp

Harmonica players

how do they do

they really

handle the harp like a pro

when they play for us

all these tones

one after another

the harmonica player plays different kind of songs

maybe it for us all that sing

along

feelings come alive and

with this little harp

the story be told

in these beautiful tones of a harp

song about blues
about the rain and the pain.
and funny songs too about
summer and love...

so, play on and on ...
don't stop now when
your harp really talks to the
spot of my heart
oh, what a great song
you offer today when
you playing with your soul this
lovely tones of today ...
all tones of a blues harp today

living

An interesting sky above
'dramatic' colour of the day
there up in the sky.
a different world beyond?
what to believe I do not know
but one day I will come to see
is it a holy heaven above or
is it just a fantasy.
one day I will come to know
but that day aren't today
because the day today
I will live every second, minutes and hours of this day
I have no time to meet the
heavenly father
I'm not rude
I just have much to do
and that is
LIVING

Aloner

You are... a loner
and that's the truth for the day
and you make it out for yourself
you always do
you are learned this way
you very good in this and
you always been
and you know selflove always
taste better than self-hate.
and comfort, love faith
just waiting for you to pick it up
for yourself
you are ... a loner
so, I think you know by yourself,
you self-decide
withs road to go today

Navigate

To navigate
you need both
'head and heart'
so, Use both, when you
navigate through your life.
let them argue
with each other
use your inner ear
and 'listen'
It can take you through
a stormy ocean, the desert...
this inner compass
help
you to
navigate
through life
just for you
to
'listen'

Truth

Look after the truth in the eyes
do you dare?
to take a closer look
what's there
on the inside
this answer hide waiting to be
found
of your sweet green eyes
so, do you dare?
to take a look
into this true-blue eye

The rain

Rain I know of it

I know how it feels

when the tears like rain

falling down the chin

I know because this tears it

was my life

all of the time for some time.

like a beautiful rain drop

there like a drop on the floor

there every drop has a

story of their own.

it sometimes feels cold

and maybe no one seems to care

but yourself

wipe it away show you care

by let it be a lonely tear drop

on the floor or let it be shared.

It's up to you, tell me about it

I'm a pro about it

I know, I know, how it feels

when rain drops fall

I think we all been there

sometimes

don't we

Scars and stiches

There are scars and there are stiches
in mine by love
tortured heart.
they all have their own story
every stich there in the
depth of my heart.
maybe you can get the permission
to hear the stories of my life
and tortured heart
only a true friend is allowed
to take a peek into
and you will find out who I am
by every stich I share
to you

The hope

When we all are in
‘the darkness’
there inside we all notice
even the smallest spark
it is Like a
‘hope’
this light
even the smallest
it
light up our dark
It
give us
h.o.p.e

yesterday

when I look into your eyes
again.
it feels like it is another
light and colour
in your eyes
than yesterdays.
something happened
through these hours
we been apart.
the love of your eyes
is gone, disappeared
from your heart.
wherever I look
I can't find it anywhere
it's gone
disappeared.
I miss the shining colour of
your eyes.
I miss the love inside
we had
and
we shared.
it's gone
and I can't find it
anywhere

Good living

When you are hungry
and your stomach scream
what you need is a good meal.
so, think with your head
and listen to the heart
that will be a good living

into your treasure chest
you can put down your gold'
banana, fruit, chicken and shrimps...
let everything you put in
lead to be a healthy life
like fish, vegetables and maybe
a little glass of red wine.
put it into your little belly
your treasure chest
and you will live a 'good life'

Beautiful morning

A

Coffee latte

into my hand.

slowly

I

'Sip it up'

it starts the day

when the sun peeking up

from the horizon line.

I'm pleased with what I got

"a beautiful morning and a

coffee cup"

Every day

When I'm in need
I try to pick it up the memories
of our sweet love
but... it gone
it has fade away, with time
our love
now it only exists in my mind
and I miss it sometimes
but I will be remembering
these good old days
when our love
Was fresh
and we lived every day
every day...

A little antique

With time
we all become
old, maybe a little antique too
Hopefully.
we be
worth more than all gold
In the world
of our own loving people

But you

One careful soft whisper
from me
into your ear.
I tell you something
you need to hear.
what it is
no one else
have permission to hear
but 'you'
my dear

Pain of yesterday

Pain of yesterdays
is gone, disappeared
where it went was into the heart
the heart takes the blame
turned it around
to
better days

Lot to do

Future you can handle
by make plans for these days.

the past you can work it out by
think it over
and
learn from your mistakes

the present you can live
this is living days
so,
do your actions well
every single day

Breakfast

Life is like a good or bad recipe
so, how it going to taste
is up to yourself
so, in this case I do my best
everyday.
I put a little sugar in it
so, it be sweet.
I put in a little pinch of salt
against the evil.
I put in a little pepper
to get a 'sting'
and a little water into too
so, it not be dry.
so, this is what I do
I mix my life recipe every day.
and don't forget... put in a little
bit of hope and trust,
truths and beliefs. Into too
so, I get that 'taste'
of life.
such a great breakfast I done
to myself
today.

Your stories

When the tears falling
they unleash you
feel free to talk say something
about it.
the tears have a story to be told
let the tear drops out of you
one by one.
let it be good, bad or glad...
history to tell to someone close
to you.
so, let the tears fall
every drop that falls have
a story of their own
so, tell your stories
you have a lot of them
so now let them come out
of you.

Beautiful hearts

You are strong and free

in your mind

with

a

strength into your soul

every day you go, go...

that's your strength, so, now you

know, know.

strong and free

choices and beliefs

to choose right way

it's your way every day

it's your strength

it makes 'you'

to who you are

every day

Golden curls

Oh!
What a sweet girl
you look like a beautiful doll
your hair has golden curls
just like a baby girl
you are the sweetest thing
I ever seen
you eat candy and have fun
in a childish
playground.
take care of the time,
time runs fast and nothing
last forever
years passing by so fast
so, play your game and have some fun
soon you grow up
from a baby to a girl
woman and a lady...
then after that you be dead
and lay in your grave
someone remembering
your name and your love
and that is
your children and friends
from your lived days
from the past

Golden heart

Be scared, be glad…

…maybe be jealous some times

be curious

on a lot of feelings

that come along all, of the time

we all have scars?!

some been there for a short while

some have fade

by love and time

we all come to know

a life isn't easy

to live sometimes.

but we still on the go, as long

as love heal the heart

everyday.

after all the feelings tortured

a heart

in good in bad

it makes the heart strong

by time.

Just like a golden heart

it shines and is a treasure

inside.

so, keep it close

and sometimes

let someone in

into the depth of your golden heart

a treasure yes, it is

and you the owner

of the key

to this golden heart

if you find someone, someone special

this key can come to be to

that someone special?!

No golden chain

In front of your eyes
is me
standing here
just like I am
I feel nude
this is all of me
real me
pure me
I pray
you like ‘me’
Just as I am
‘Me’
and
not for my golden chain
so
I show you pure me
my soul
nude
for you to see
today

Weather reports

Love and the weather
It's like the same
It's weather reports
for every day

the weather conditions
can Change all of the time

weather condition
say?!
how will it be
tomorrow day?

A gentleman

You are a talking
kind of man
but you also know
“a gentleman knows when to talk
and when
to close his mouth”

Aquarium

To be a fish
seems nice to be
but inside the aquarium
it's a hierarchy
so, to be a little fish
is harder
then it seems to be

Time goes by

She used

to love you, everything with you

but that days is gone

these days.

now you can only find

'the loss'

that is all what's remain

in the depth of your heart

you miss the love you had

but sometimes

nothing last

it's So sad

it fades away

when time goes by

Living

Its like I'm living on the edge
I give everything
and take everything
I can get

If we need, we all can heal
with love from a warm heart
I had the luck to find it
yesterday
in someone I met

I want to be that friend today
and give a piece of heart
to someone else this day

we all understand we all need to
meet this kind of 'man'
some days
so, let me be that 'man'
for you
today

memory

A beautiful day

sunshine and your beautiful blue eyes

it is a beautiful mix

of this summer day

you smile so quietly

to me

It's for real

when you smile

so sweet to me

Oh! This

beautiful memory

Bee

Now you are angry
like a bee
when I said
goodbye
to you from me
trouble
in my head
calculation says
I'm dead
if I don't
say sorry to you
from me
in another way
so, you accept my need
to be free
so, calm down little bee
it exists other flowers
then me

Songs of life

Wonder of life
is in my mind
when
words never end
its
always a new line
to be found
for me to listen on
music is life
written
for everyone
this
Oh!
Songs of life

Key

Something

lay protected

in the depth of the heart

it's

love

respect it.

the rule to get this key

to the door

of this heart

'Is a secret'

and

'Secret of a heart'

need a key

when it protected of me

what's the key

Its

'Me

love me'

Necklace

This
necklace
a gift
from my heart
to you to wear around your neck
and
close to your heart
will it do?
my present to you
let me know
when I give it to you
I see it in your eyes
and your act
If you wear it
will my present be
something to you
or
is it just
mean
nothing
to you

Try again

Love can lose its glory
with time
we can lose the glow
what we do with it then
s.o.s into our hearts
and our souls
you used to be... my oxygen.
I'm used to be... your fire.
so, if we give it time
and a new try
we start to love
each other again
try again

In your eyes

I fall...

fall and fall...

into the depth of your eyes

I find it so deep

It makes me notice I really 'love'

your eyes.

I fall and fall into the depth of

your beautiful blue eyes

let me fall

let me be alive

let me fall deep, deep

into your eyes.

let me live one more day

it feels like everything else is

a waste of time

I’m left

Love was
but
that was yesterdays
today it feels gone
can’t find it in your eyes
anymore.
I’m left. you gone
scared to be this alone
love feels dangerous
when it changeably
but that how life can be
that’s life, follow the flow
love to eternity
or let it all go

When time is tough

Sometimes it feels
like the
morning light
comes to soon
when I need more time
to rest my mind and soul
in this world
of a new dawn
exist the need of a gift
of a rest
for my mind and soul
with longer nights
and
shorter days
I feel alright
when time is tough

I'm here

I'm here it's me
I think of you
where ever you be
you in my heart
I hope to see or hear
from you soon
when you are in need
I hope
you think of me
knowing I'm here
for you
always
because I love you
forever
I do
hope you know it
it's true

Live your life

Live and tell

you get paid later

In heaven or hell

Woman and a man

A woman and a man
from day one
they were the 'one'
listen to their story
as many years passing by
world roll around
and they still stand as 'one'
hearts pounding in their chest
all secrets they hide
and their story together
deep inside
the story of their life
married many years
Oh! This life
the story
and history
of a woman and a man
as a
husband and wife

Know

You

Just

'know'

when it's for real

Understand

You make some noise
in my ear, your abc...
it makes me understand

so, tell me a line
understand?

Story of my heart

you just dropped in

here you have a place

you are now a part

of this story

of my heart

Tarot

Sometimes life can be hard
for everyone
then
I need to see
take a little look
into the
beautiful
old
'Pack of cards'
of
'Tarot'
when life is hard
I wish a good card
telling me
something real
Oh! Little card
you
tell me
something
deep
you

lay the ground
for the road
to me
to walk
so, now it's time
to pick a card
I lay and read
out my card
to make me through
the day
and
get an answer
for this day
I'm
with love
reading
what's written
Into the open card
I must
Just dare
to read
if it's a
'scary card'

Monday again

The man
drinking a coke
with a friend
In a bar
they dance on the floor
& playing some cards
in this
wanted weekend
days go fast away
when it's fun
soon its time
for a
Monday
again

For you

Please don't say it out loud
my love for you
It's true
but I'm not ready
to stand in the light
about you
so please be careful what you say & do
I'm not ready on any way
Just wait a little while
soon I stand steady
and turn up
the light
about my love
for you
my love
soon

You are

When tomorrow never come
you lonesome
on this lonely road
you on
again
your darling left you
you on your own
so, a good friend tells you
love can rebirth itself
so, you find yourself
once again
Just give love
to yourself
then people see
a heart so true
they will want you
as you are
when they see
what a masterpiece
you are
scars, love, maturity

and everything

within you

like a beautiful painting

you are

The way

Lost
In the dark
of a broken heart
turn up the light
in my soul
let love live into my heart
again
let me see
the way
through
for this broken heart
love can rebirth itself
Just find the way
love is the biggest thing
I say
it makes me survive a lonely day
Just help me
find the way

Red balloon

You and your kind eyes
you looking at me
your heart is big
like a red balloon
I can always count on you
thank you

Life

Life
passes by so fast with time
I think.
be old and wise at last
grow grey, grow wise, grow old
with dignity hopefully
with time see things
differently
find love magickly
no longer waste time
with stupidity
take time
to think it over
what I did back then
is not what I do again
wise like the owl
say hi
to solutions easier than war
you see it's not like
Before
when I must have right

with the

price of war

it's an art

to go old

with peace and happiness

and feel young until the end of time

it's all about to live

and end it

nice

peace of all I think we all

looking for

in the end

take a last breath

find

peace

into your soul

Every day

Everyday Life is a gift
if you
handle it with care.

One more day
I hopefully find you here again
by my side

thanks for your time
every minute,
every second...
...every day

I don't want to be
without you
you are everything
In this world
to me
you are
my oxygen
I need it
to breath it
everyday

Friendly advice

Need a telephone
to put me on the line
to get me some talking time
with a friend
of mine
will he/she answer the phone
when I call, he/she answers on the
private line
when I
ring the bell
need some answers
and advice for my life
day like this
don't be too shy
when life is about
to live a life
have my friend answers for my life
when I call on and on
On my friend's telephone
will I get
what I need
will I get
some
friendly
good
advice

Traveling people& memories

To

make some life out of a day

you can

Just

put some dollar

on the wheels, plane

bus or train...

you will see

happiness

endlessly

with

'Traveling people'

everywhere

finding and

making

'Some memories'

I want to be there

I want to be there
for you
in rain
in shine
in darker days
and often when you smile
want to share
the moments of life
in every day
what about that
Say?

'Only you'

It's like a darkness
It twisted into my
thoughts and mind.
and inside my mind
this black feeling just grow
and grow
It's a dark day into my soul
something turned off the light
so, I can't see the 'spark'
of life, today
what I need is you and
your loving light
but you gone
It's like the season change
from a warm summer day
to a cold blow winter night
you are dead
laying in your grave.
and nothing can comfort me
but you
only you
but you are gone
and
this is the blackiest day
I ever felt in my life

Man

Yesterdays...
...I was just a boy.
but I woke up
from
this childish playground

when...
then
'I become a man'
with
this 'transformations' within
my thoughts,
into my mind, heart and soul
make me to who I am, today
a man

and with my head high up
in a clear blue sky
and my feet on the steady ground
I stand ready n' steady
with my new wishes...
and thoughts

...of a man

Summer season, once again

Sorrow, pain, hurt, anger
Sadness, anxious...
Is it possible for me to say
Goodbye to them? To be free?
I think if I put them down in the
hole, in the cold ground
I let all this 'heavy feelings'
sleep in this grave
instead of myself.

Farewell darkness

Goodbye of misery

When the 'bad feeling' is buried
In this black hole down in the
ground
it gives peace to my troubled mind
and peace to this
'bad feelings'

that laying twisted

deep down in the ground.

.. later after some months the

summer start to 'talk' again on the

green grass on this grave a little

flower force itself up

it's summer season' once again

it tells us all- life is strong

the flower shows us-

love to life

is

stronger than death.